Rivka's First Thanksgiving

Written by Elsa Okon Rael

Illustrated by Maryann Kovalski

Margaret K. McElderry Books

NEW YORK LONDON TORONTO SYDNEY SINGAPORE

For Lynne Okon Scholnick, beloved sister and friend

—E. R.

For those who came before me, who came from there

—M. K.

Margaret K. McElderry Books
An imprint of Simon & Schuster Children's Publishing Division
1230 Avenue of the Americas
New York, NY 10020

Book design by Ann Bobco and Kristin Smith
The text of this book was set in Centaur MT.
The illustrations were rendered in colored pencil and acrylics.
Printed in Hong Kong

1 2 3 4 5 6 7 8 9 10
Library of Congress Cataloging-in-Publication Data

Rael, Elsa Okon.
Rivka's first Thanksgiving / Elsa Okon Rael ; illustrated by Maryann Kovalski—1st ed.
p. cm.
Summary: Having heard about Thanksgiving in school, nine-year-old Rivka tries to convince her
immigrant family and her Rabbi that it is a holiday for all Americans, Jews and non-Jews alike.
ISBN 0-689-83901-4
[Thanksgiving Day—Fiction. Jews—United States—Fiction. Immigrants—Fiction.]
I. Kovalski, Maryann, ill. II. Title.

PZ7.R1235 Ri 2001
[E]—dc21
00-058738

Author's Note

The idea for *Rivka's First Thanksgiving* came from a shared family memory. At a recent Passover seder, I recalled my family's first Thanksgiving. It was in public school, when I was in second or third grade, that I first learned about the Pilgrims and the Native Americans. As Jewish immigrants from Poland, my parents had never heard of Thanksgiving, but I managed to convince them that the holiday was a celebration for *all* Americans, Jews and non-Jews alike. When I recounted this memory I was surprised at how clearly each of my cousins remembered bringing home the same information from school! My cousin Shirley recalled that her mother, my Tante Sylvie, replied, "That sounds nice, but what's a turkey?"

Today, immigrants from diverse cultures around the world continue to arrive in this wonderful country, which the Jewish people call the *Goldeneh Medinah* (the Golden Haven). Like Rivka, the children of these immigrants are learning about Thanksgiving in school and teaching their families about this uniquely American festival. It's a pleasure to share with you the story of one child's first Thanksgiving in a new homeland.

—Elsa Okon Rael

"That's a funny-looking *kotchka*," Mama said, peering over Rivka's shoulder at her colored pencil sketch.

"It's not a duck, Mama," Rivka replied, returning to her drawing. "It's a turkey to celebrate Thanksgiving."

"What's Thanksgiv—" Mama started to ask, but was interrupted when Rivka's grandmother rushed into the apartment with a jar of hot applesauce. She looked over Rivka's shoulder and said, "That's a funny-looking *kotchka*, Rivkeleh."

"It's a turkey, Bubbeh. For school. We're learning about Thanksgiving."

Bubbeh looked at Mama for an explanation, but Mama shrugged her shoulders to show she didn't know, either. "Thanksgiving? What is it?" asked Bubbeh.

"It's a big, happy holiday to celebrate the friendship between the Indians and the Pilgrims. It's an important holiday, and I think we should celebrate it, too!"

"But we don't know any Indians," Bubbeh said. "Do we?"

"It sounds to me as though this is a party for Gentiles," Mama added. "It's not for us."

"You're wrong, Mama. It started with the Indians, because they helped the Pilgrims build houses and plant crops. So, to thank the Indians for helping, and to thank God for bringing them to this wonderful country, the Pilgrims made a celebration, a feast, and they called it Thanksgiving."

Mama looked doubtful.

"It's true, Mama. Miss Broderick said Thanksgiving is a *national* holiday. For everybody."

"But it can't be for us," Bubbeh said. "It's not for Jews, or we would know about it."

"Thanksgiving is for all Americans, Bubbeh. Aren't we Americans, too?"

Bubbeh and Mama exchanged flustered looks, then Bubbeh announced, "In the morning I'll go to Rivington Street." This meant Bubbeh planned to consult with the Rabbi Yoshe Preminger.

That night, when Papa came home, Mama asked if he'd ever heard of Thanksgiving.

"It's a holiday," he said. "A family holiday with a lot of food."

"Is it for Jews?" Mama asked.

"I don't know," Papa admitted. "The teacher in my English class didn't say anything about religion. She told us the early Americans made a harvest festival and they called it Thanksgiving. That's what I remember."

When Rivka came home from school the next day, Bubbeh was waiting for her. "Don't take off your coat," she said excitedly. "The Rabbi Yoshe Preminger wants to see you, to talk to you."

"Why?" Rivka had never met the esteemed Rabbi Yoshe Preminger, and she was a little frightened at the idea.

"Why? Because the Tsaddik said for you to come. That's why." For Bubbeh, no further explanation was needed.

As they walked up the steep, creaking flight of stairs to the Rabbi's
apartment on Rivington Street, Rivka smelled the rotting wood of the
old tenement building. Bubbeh rapped on the door softly.

Almost immediately, the Rebbetzin Preminger, wearing a black wavy *sheitl* over her hair, welcomed them in. She smiled and put her index finger to her lips as she led them down the long hallway to Rabbi Yoshe Preminger's study. She knocked twice on the door.

"Come," said a voice from inside.

The room was dark and musty. Books lined all four walls and were stacked on the windowsill, so that little light penetrated the room.

Behind the desk sat a very small, white-bearded man. Rivka thought he looked like a gnome on a throne. But the deep voice that came from the Rabbi Yoshe Preminger belied his size.

"So," he boomed, "you are a Jewish child?"

"Yes, Rabbi."

"How old are you?"

"Nine years old, Rabbi."

"You are a good student? You listen to your parents? You don't gossip or lie?"

"She is a good child, Rabbi," Bubbeh assured him. "In every way."

"Good. So tell me about this . . . celebration, this Thanksgiving. Is this a celebration that would please the Almighty-blessed-be-He?"

"It's a celebration to honor the Almighty, Rabbi . . . to give thanks for being here in America."

"And you believe Jews have much for which to be thankful?"

"Yes! Oh, yes, Rabbi. Here in America we do. In parts of Europe, terrible things happen to Jews every day—riots and pogroms. My father told me of the horrible things that are happening there right now. But here we are safe. I wish all Jews in Europe could come here, don't you, Rabbi?"

The Rabbi's voice softened. "Indeed," he said, nodding his head. "Indeed, you make an argument I will consider. But I shall have to learn more about your Thanksgiving before I render a comment. Meanwhile, go in good health."

Two days later, Bubbeh told Rivka that the Rabbi Yoshe Preminger
had decided Thanksgiving was not a celebration for Jews. For Mama
and Bubbeh, the last word had been given: no Thanksgiving.

For several days, Rivka fretted. The Rabbi's decision was wrong!
She would have to tell him. She wrote a letter and walked to
Rivington Street. Her heart was pounding as she slipped the
letter under the Rabbi's front door and dashed away.

To the Rabbi Yoshe Preminger, Sir,

My Bubbeh believes you are the wisest man in the whole world, but I cannot agree with her. You may have read a thousand books, but you do not seem to understand that immigrants came to America to escape from mean, wicked people who hurt them and their families. That is why the Pilgrims came and that is why the Jewish people came later. The Pilgrims were thankfull and I think that we should be too.

Signed by
Rivka Rabin

The very next day, Bubbeh told Rivka that the Rabbi Yoshe
Preminger wanted to see her again.

"Why?" Rivka asked anxiously.

"Why? Because the Tsaddik said for you to come. That's why."

Was the Rabbi going to punish her? Rivka worried that her legs
wouldn't carry her to Rivington Street and up the steep flight of stairs.
By the time they arrived, she was breathless with fear. When the
Rebbetzin opened the door, she whispered that Bubbeh was to come into
the kitchen for tea while Rivka met with the Rabbi.

Oh, what had she done? Why had she written that letter?
What would the Rabbi do to her?

Rivka shook as she entered the Rabbi's study. There sat *seven* bearded men! The air was stifling. Rivka thought she might faint. The Rabbi introduced each of the men by name and title, but Rivka didn't hear. Then the Rabbi announced, "This is the child for whom I convened this assembly." Addressing Rivka, he asked, "Will you please tell the learned Rabbis what you told me?"

"I'm sorry I wrote you that rude letter, Rabbi," Rivka squeaked.

"It sometimes takes a little rudeness to accomplish what we attempt. Now, tell them. Speak. About this Thanksgiving."

"Oh . . . I . . . yes . . . Thanksgiving. It's an American holiday." Then, still quivering, she looked directly at the men and said, "It's a celebration that *all* Americans can share. We are here, in this wonderful country, and for that we should be thankful."

"I was lucky to be born here, but my mother and her parents came from Buchach. My bubbeh says you also came from Buchach, Rabbi, so you must know about the terrible pogroms there. They happened all the time, for no reason. My mother was badly hurt in a pogrom when she was twelve years old. A cossack on a horse struck her on the head because she was Jewish—for no other reason than that. No one thought she would live, but she did. She can't remember anything that happened to her before she was twelve. Nothing. Not a single thing."

The Rabbis shook their heads sadly.

"So here we are now, safe in America. God first brought the Pilgrims and then He brought us, the Jews. The Pilgrims were the first to give thanks to Him, but I believe we also owe Him a Thanksgiving. As much as anybody, we owe Him thanks."

One of the Rabbis leaned forward and asked, "In what manner is this thanks given?"

"From what my teacher told me, it sounds something like a seder, Rabbi. Family and friends sit down together, offer a prayer of thanks, and then they eat together."

Two weeks later, Rivka served the food for the first Thanksgiving on Hester Street.

Bubbeh had roasted a turkey—her first. There were sweet potatoes, salads, coleslaw, green beans, challah, and mandel-brodt, which was a specialty of Mama's. Rivka, who'd gotten the recipe from her teacher, made cranberry sauce.

The table was set with Mama's prettiest party dishes, and wineglasses that sparkled in the candlelight.

The Rabbi Yoshe Preminger sat at the head of the table,
surrounded by Rivka's whole family—Mama, Papa, and baby
Sorreh; Bubbeh and Zaydeh; Tante Golda and Uncle Moishe, and
Rivka's three cousins, Saul, Muttie, and Zeesie. The Rabbi said a
prayer in Hebrew, which Rivka thought must be a long thank-you,
and everyone said "Amen." Then he looked at Rivka.

"It is also a great pleasure to give my heartfelt thanks to the Almighty-blessed-be-He, for the wisdom children give us."

Rivka blushed happily.

Papa carved the turkey, and Bubbeh passed Rivka the very first slice.

Beaming, Bubbeh said, "I'm also grateful to
Him-blessed-be-He, for my smart granddaughter.
Eat, Rivkeleh, eat. And happy Thanksgiving."

Glossary

bubbeh (BUB-eh) — grandmother *(Yiddish)*

Buchach (boo-CHUTCH) — a small town in Poland *(Polish)*

challah (CHOLL-ah) — a braided, white, egg bread traditionally eaten by Jews on the Sabbath and holidays *(Yiddish)*

cossack (KOS-ak) — a Russian soldier or horseman *(Russian)*

kotchka (KOCH-ka) — duck *(Yiddish)*

mandel-brodt (MON-del broyt) — a semisweet bread-cake, usually with almonds *(Yiddish)*

Passover — the eight-day holiday celebrating the Jews' escape from slavery in Egypt 3,200 years ago *(English)*

pogrom (po-GRUM) — an organized persecution or massacre *(Yiddish)*

Rebbetzin (REB-etz-in) — a Rabbi's wife *(Yiddish)*

Rivka (RIV-ka) — Yiddish variant of the Hebrew name Rebecca, meaning "bound" *(Yiddish)*

Rivkeleh (RIV-kell-eh) — Little Rivka *(Yiddish)*

seder (SAY-der) — the ceremonial Passover dinner during which the story of the Jews' escape from slavery in Egypt is told. Symbolic foods are eaten in addition to the regular meal. *(Hebrew)*

sheitl (SHY-tl; SHAY-tl) — ritual wig worn by Orthodox Jewish women *(Yiddish)*

tante (TON-teh) — aunt *(Yiddish)*

tsaddik (TSA-dik) — a completely righteous individual and learned scholar *(Yiddish)*

Yoshe (YUSH-eh; YOSH-eh) — a male first name, meaning "Jehovah's gift" *(Yiddish and Hebrew)*

zaydeh (ZAY-deh) — grandfather *(Yiddish)*